Pop! Pop! Pop!

Written by Joe Elliot

Illustrated by Neil Sutherland, Blue-Zoo and Tony Trimmer

 o nods.

 **p** pops in.

t-**o**-**p**, top!

m-**o**-**p**, mop!

4

p-**o**-**p**, pop!

p-**o**-**t**, pot!

Stop!  o can not kip.

c-o-t , cot!

 pops in to a cot. kips.